copyright

I0625573

INCOMPLETE WITHOUT HER

© 2017 Urquhart Randolph

A NEW ROMANCE NOVEL

Published by Glofton llc

DISCLAIMER

This is a work of fiction. Names, characters, organizations, spots, occasions and occurrences are either the results of the creator's creative energy or utilized as a part of an invented way. Any similarity to real people, living or dead, or genuine occasions is absolutely adventitious.

ISBN:

EBook: 978-1-946792-06-8
print:978-1-946792-07-5
audio/d: 978-1-946792-08-2

© **2017 Urquhart Randolph**

Published by Glofton llc

All rights held. No some portion of this production might be replicated, dispersed, or transmitted in any shape or by any methods, including photocopying, recording, or other electronic or mechanical strategies, without the earlier composed authorization of the distributer, aside from on account of brief citations encapsulated in basic audits and certain other noncommercial uses allowed by copyright law.

.

copyright

TABLE OF CONTENT

VISIT US
WWW.GLOFTON.COM
Enroll in our VIP list.
Be the first to be notified on our latest published book.
Downloading for free gifts.

copyright

Guitar as a padlock

Chapter 1

If there's something that I want to say about rock 'n roll then it would be one word - silence. A silence of brain, while the heart is carrying out the easy work of putting out everything that hurts, getting a feeling of relief during such emotional expression. For me, it was hard to be understood.

People I worked with didn't really understand my way of living. This time was for them a time when they should enjoy their life as much as possible. " I want to live while I'm young, I want to enjoy the life as much as possible while I'm young", almost every of my coworkers used to say this.

It seems like emotions are buried down during this period of life. Inhale the smoke of a cigarette, get drunk as fuck, and fuck something by the end of the night, would make a perfect day for them. I enjoy the cigarettes too; sex is even better" But what about abstract things one can derive joy

copyright

from?" - I asked while we were talking in a park after we had an exhausting football game.

"Carl, not again with your stupid shit", Said Bart while looking at the ground, having his hands in his pocket and making a jingling noise with coins inside of it.

"What about hanging out with us tonight, maybe you get some" - said Nick

"All right, I'll go." I was thinking myself that it would be the best to live the life they live until I get a bit closer to them, and at the end make them realize that not everything is about going to clubs.

Anyway, I went out with them that night, and I ended up in a bed with a beautiful girl, at the end of the romance, she asked "Why don't you stay a bit longer?", and as I wanted to keep with the attitudes of my friends, I decided to leave, which of course, she didn't like. "You're already leaving?" Sophia said while I was putting my pants on. I got dressed and I left without a word said. I worked as a psychotherapist in a hospital. Since I was good with playing guitar, I had a special treatment which was based on singing songs to the patients that they enjoyed the most.

They would name a song that makes them feel relief, and we would sing it together. As I spent more and more time with my friends getting drunk every night and ending up with a different girl every night, I became more and more insensitive.

Unconditional love conditioned by her flaws

Chapter 2

Living just like another snowflake, I was in a motion, but I didn't know what land to fly down.

I remember that special day when a female patient opened the door and just with her head peeking, she asked if she can come in.

"Yes, Of Course," I said while I was rearranging documents that I previously reviewed. She had the most beautiful hair in the world.

"My name is Emma"

copyright

"I'm Carl. Emma, take a seat please."

"They are after me."

"Who is after you?" I said while looking at her red hair more than I looked in her eyes.

"Wolves, I feel that they will come out every moment."

"You spend a lot of time in woods, do you?"

"I never go to woods, I live here, in the city of New York. Why are you asking that?" She said in a curious manner.

"Well, we will really have to work on this, since you are not able to distinguish what is rational from what isn't."

I was constantly looking at her hair. Noticing that I look at her that way, and somehow with a fire in her eyes, she was looking at my guitar while biting her lip.

"You play guitar?"

"Well, I play guitar, and I do it good. I will not be treating you with the guitar since your problem requires different approach."

copyright

"What approach? What about me approaching you a little bit closer?"

"Excuse me?" I cough.

"I see that you play guitar, I love gentle guys. You are a complete contrast from the wolves, they are angry, inflicting pain. I don't know much about psychology but I differentiate two kinds of pain: the pain that I won't longer feel if you do your job well, and pain that I love, the one that you will make me feel." She unbuttoned one button of her shirt and she put a hand on her breast.

"All right, I see what you want, but we must go out of here, we can't do it here, someone could catch us"

I grabbed her hand and led her to my car.

Next fifteen minutes in the rear view mirror our bodies were reflected from different angles.

"I will never be growling at you." I said as I was kissing her body, from her occiput to her heel. I was touching each of her feminine beautiful parts. I was kissing her hair most of the time. I made her love while we were lying

copyright

between front seats, having our heads touching gear box. She was screaming " Harder, Harder", which is what I did. She almost passed out but we made it to the end.

She said she has never felt better. The smoke of the cigarette covered my car, while we were lying, me smoking my cigarette, and she kissing my tattooed shoulder.

I wanted to have this woman in my life. I fell in love. I started writing songs for her. She said she never had someone like me in her life. Two years passed by, and our relationship was so strong that I couldn't imagine her not being my partner. I worked on her problem, but results were very bad. She said that fear from the wolves emerged when she was 23.

The fear started after she watched some documentary movie about animals.

She watched a scene where two wolves were jumping on the edges of a cage, trying to climb to the top wanting to escape the cage, which was impossible because the cage was completely closed. After a failure to succeed in their escape, wolves would get off the edge where they've previously been at,

copyright

and each of them would run to different edges, intersecting their ways. She believed that this had to do something with her future.

Life may look harsh, but neither the ground is to be underestimated

Chapter 3

Emma and I decided to have a party. She had a huge house and we invited almost 70 people. During the ride to one of her friends, according to her words, she noticed that the ground is moving, but not as the earthquake. She said that it was like a wave rising and coming back. I looked, but couldn't see anything, looking at it too long made me pass over to a wrong track of the road, which led to an accident. The car was wrecked and smoke was all over the car. This time the smoke wasn't from a cigarette

I held one hand at my ribs while I placed another hand on her neck to see if I can feel the pulse. She was alive. I took out the mobile from my pocket and I called the ambulance. As soon as they arrived my dear was away

copyright

together with nurses, siren and a few tears that I shed on her beautiful hair. I was in a shock, but the guy that I hit with my car didn't care about that.

"I'm sorry that all of this happens to you, but somebody has to pay for the damage done to my car."

He wasn't injured, but his car was damaged.

Police came and a fat officer got out of a car. He was holding a small notebook along with a pen in his hand.

"Well. Seems like we're going have a lot of work today Olivia", Said the policemen while caressing his mustache.

"Yeah, this is a third time this month that we were interrupted during a lunch."

He approached me.

"What happened?"

"My girlfriend said that ground is moving..." As soon as I said this policeman started laughing like crazy.

copyright

"Ground started moving? I am working for 20 years as a policeman, but I've never seen the stupidest attempt to deceive a policeman"

"No sir, I'm not trying to deceive you, I admit that I am guilty here.

"Man, your girlfriend might be having some issues she should work on because we don't often see that ground is moving, do we, Olivia?"

"Definitely not, sir." Answered Olivia waving her hand and therefore showing that she also thinks it was a nonsense. I was thinking the same until something changed my mind after the accident happened.

After just a few minutes, some guy came up and he took a picture of the cars and everything. Every picture had a sound of a thunder.

I couldn't believe it was happening to me. I resolved the issue with the police, and during the long process, I had to pay a substantial sum of money for what I did. Besides all the sorrow in me, I wasn't

copyright

depressed. The thing that was keeping me alive was the moving ground. I knew that Emma had the phobia, but she never mentioned any hallucinations. I was sent to a hospital to get my broken rib healed. While entering the room, I saw a doctor with his back turned to me

At the hospital

Chapter 4

"Doctor!" I shouted

A bold man with beard turned, took my hand rapidly and led me to a room.

"Wait there." Said the doctor. After 10 minutes of waiting, a nurse finally came and took a care of me. She said that I must be resting and that I must not make sudden moves. In the same hospital was Emma, I went to the second floor and as I walked closer to her room I felt bigger pressure in my heart. I had a lot of fears when I was dealing with important things.

copyright

As an example, the first time I was on a stage, singing a song for the first time, my hands were shaking and my head was covered with sweat. The first time I was treating a patient I was stuttering. I stuttered so much that in a middle of the conversation patient asked me if I need a help.

But the first time I met her, I was the happiest man alive, our bodies merged, our sweat was of the same impurity, our lust at the same intensity, and our tongues fighting the lust.

I was scared, scared to death to see her dead. I didn't want that time to be the last time that I was going see her.

I've dedicated too many songs to her to write one last song which would make me a relief. I didn't want to be my own patient, I didn't want my heart to carry out the easy work of putting out everything that hurts, getting a feeling of relief during such emotional expression. I didn't want that because this time I wasn't sure if it was going to be easy.

copyright

I cried. They say that man should not cry and I ask why? I wouldn't say that a sign of masculinity is hiding your emotions, and later behaving wrongfully to someone who doesn't deserve that just because the man had to throw out that negative energy that was left in him when he refused to cry. If he cried, he wouldn't have insulted his wife, nor would he have to walk the whole day without a smile on his face.

As I reached the doors, a doctor came in my way and said:

"What are you up for?"

"I'm here to see my girlfriend. Tell me, is she okay?"

"What's your name?"

"My name is Carl."

"I'm doctor James. It's nice to see that you care about your wife. But nobody can enter this room."

"She's not my wife. She is my girlfriend. I must get into that room; I must see if she is better. Doctor, let me in."

copyright

"No way, the rules are same for everyone."

"At least, tell me if she's better?"

The doctor shrugged as he started walking away from me.

"If she survives until the morning, chances are that her condition will be getting better and better."

Despite the prohibition, I entered the room where Emma was. I approached her, I sat myself down, and for the next five minutes, I was just looking at her beautiful face. Her face looked so tired, so tired that I though hospital will fall asleep. I put her hand in my hand, and it felt incredibly good.

"Do you remember when wind crossed your hair adhering yellow pedals to your red hair, the pedals that I tore from a rose. I know that sometimes I acted like I don't care, but I cared more than ever, and this car crash I will forgive myself never.

You are the definition of positiveness, I've never seen the happiest person with so many

copyright

problems. Your face is so peaceful that silence dances to a noisy music in your presence.

Even when I didn't know you, I knew that you were someone worth of getting to know. You picked up two separated pieces of my heart, put them together and weaved happiness. If you pass away, I just want to say that I'm sorry for not being able to cure you. I know how badly you wanted to get rid of the phobia."

I pulled out a yellow rose that I held under my shirt.

"This is for you. I know that I used to throw these into the air, letting it come up to your hair, but today is a little bit different situation. There is no wind, and we're not as happy as we were back then. I'm leaving this rose here, and I hope that tomorrow you will open your eyes, and enjoy the aroma of this rose, just as I enjoyed your presence in my life". I went to my house and I tried to sleep. I closed my eyes after 3 hours of sleep. I awoke next day at 8 a.m. and I headed to the hospital. When I came into the hospital entered the room where Emma was. When I

copyright

opened the doors, I saw her lying in her bed staring at the wall. I approached her immediately and I hugged her. She pushed me away with her hands.

"Help me!" She shouted.

I was extremely happy that she was alive, but I didn't know what happens with her.

"Sweetheart, what's the problem, are you angry?" I said this as a doctor entered the room. Since this wasn't the doctor from the day before, he thought that I was some kind of maniac and he grabbed me from my back holding my both hands.

"Who are you?" Shouted the doctor.

"I'm her boyfriend, leave me alone. Isn't that right, Emma?"

"Get this man out of this room. I don't know him and I don't want him in this room". Said Emma.

Standing alone in front of the hospital I wondered what's going on.

copyright

Searching for relaxation in a place that leads to hell

Chapter 5

Either she lost her memory, or she is angry after what happened.

I didn't know what to think. I went to an old pub where I used to spend the time before I met Emma.

"A whiskey."

"I'm sorry, what do you want?"

"One whiskey, please. Is it now okay, Edward?"

"I'm joking pal, everything for you, my friend," Sad Edward while pouring up a glass of whiskey.

"What's on your mind?" He added.

"The whole weight of the world."

"Is it so bad?"

"Even worse."

"Someone died?"

copyright

"No, but Emma could've been dead now."

Edward stopped sweeping the bar and he took a sharp look at me.

"What do you mean?"

"We had a car accident. I broke my rib only, but she was unconscious for the whole night. I am glad that she survived, but she doesn't want to talk to me.

She says that she doesn't know me, and I'm not sure if she is saying that because she's angry or because she lost her memory. I didn't have enough time to find out."

"How come you didn't have enough time to find out?"

"She said that she wants me to leave the hospital, and I didn't want to stay if she doesn't want it."

"Okay, but while would she be angry at you?"

"I was driving when the car accident happened."

copyright

"But you didn't do it intentionally, did you?"

"Of Course I didn't, Edward, but I had a responsibility to keep her safe when she's with me."

"Anyway, what exactly happened? What have you crashed into?"

"We crashed into a blue car. I passed over to a wrong track of the road."

"Why? Were you drunk?"

"No. There was something that I was looking for outside the road. Never mind."

"What is it?" Edward asked while looking at me in a curious manner as he was looking at the sun falling.

"Never mind." I said while nodding my head as if I wanted to say that it doesn't matter.

"I insist!"

"But you will laugh"

"I will not laugh."

copyright

"Yes, you will!"

"No, I will not laugh, didn't I say that?" Said Edward, as he hit the bar with his hand.

"So that is the way you talk to your friend? I'm leaving this pub, have a nice day treating someone else like that, not me."

Just as I leaned the glass of whiskey on my lips and let few drops come into my mouth, Edward said something that I will never forget

"Ground isn't always like that?" Mumbled Edward

As soon as he said that I spat out the whiskey from my mouth.

I didn't care about what I've just done. I was looking at Edward as he was looking at me. He had his mouth half-opened, and his eyes were wide.

An expression of regret was obvious on his face.

"Wait, wait, wait. What's that, that you know?" Just as I've said this, a man so drunk that he walked like a zombie, came to the bar

copyright

and having his lips raised almost to his nose with hands in his pocket he started mumbling.

"What's this, is this how you welcome people in your bar? What's this mess all about? Give me that bear – He pointed with his finger at a fridge."

"We don't serve bears here, only beers." Said Edward, as he laughed.

"I'm a bit drunk so I have some problems with talking, don't make fun of me. You fat polar bear, give me some beer, otherwise, I'm leaving the pub immediately."

Just as he said this, Edward's face went red and he vigorously jumped over the bar and punched the drunk man two times in his head.

Edward was shaking his hand looking at the drunk man. The man was lying on his back. The man raised up his hand a little bit tapping the floor with his fingers. Since the pub was big, they had two guards securing it. Both of them grabbed the man and they threw him out.

copyright

Edward was a little bit fat, but he didn't want to be called like that.

"Epic, just Epic." Said Edward, while he was wiping the bar with a rag.

"Yeah, it's epic that you are wiping that bar with the rag, although this is a big pub with a rich owner."

"The same owner might fire me after what I've just done. Anyway, shits."

"What shits? Can you talk clearly? Maybe the man you hit frightened you?" I said while I was laughing.

"Don't you wind me up, Carl. Shit that happens in this pub is epic. Every day you meet a new fool. Well, I'm not taking you into account, you are an old fool." He said as he was laughing arrogantly

"Look, you must tell me about the moving ground!" I said as I was putting my both hands on the slippery bar, right after he wiped a part of the bar where my glass was placed.

copyright

"I was just joking; I don't know anything about any ground." He didn't look in my eyes. It was obvious that he was hiding something.

"Look, you're stubborn. You're behaving like a child. I'm leaving now, but one day you will have to tell me about the ground."

"You're tripping, man." Said Edward, as I was closing the doors of the pub and leaving the place.

Unexpected direction of bullets

Chapter 6

Since a local service was repairing my car I had to walk to home by foot.

Every day was black. Even when the sun was shining, for me it was all black. I was painting magpies. Painting those birds was making me peaceful. I was thinking about life and the black color that I was painting them with, used to portray my condition.

I would put the pictures in my room. The room was big so I could arrange a lot of

copyright

pictures. They were aligned from one end to another end of the room. Looking through a window of my room, I was singing songs.

One day, as I played with electric guitar and as I was making a loud sound, someone made even a louder sound. Bullets of gun penetrated into my pictures, in every picture, except the one that I was unintentionally covering with my body, since it was behind me while I was singing. After all that happened, someone comes to shoot my paintings, to shoot the space around birds, as it wanted to say: "Don't leave that white space in your picture above the bird's head. Your life isn't empty, it's filled with black, so don't disrespect your pictures."

I was scared to death.

"Well, It seems like one picture is left right there, behind you."

I left the guitar on the floor and I turned to the doors of the room. I saw Edward standing right there with a gun in his right hand.

copyright

"Take it easy friend, just take it easy. I'll give you anything you want, just don't do anything stupid."

"I'm here to kill the bird behind you, I'm not going to do any harm to you. Why would I do it? But something deep inside me tells me that you must not move while I shoot the bird you painted. You know, it's not that I want to hurt you, as you can see, I shot the pictures only. I don't like magpies, that's all."

Edward stripped off his jacket and hung it on a chair. He was looking at my eyes when chair-creak interrupted the silence, as he sat down on the chair. He put his gun on the floor and he lighted a cigarette. He put a lighter in the box where he held cigarettes, just enough of the space was left in the box so he could put the lighter inside. After he put it, not even a toothpick was capable of fitting in the box. He put the box of cigarettes on the floor and he pushed it in a way that it ended up right by my legs.

"I'm sorry for not letting you choose your last wish. But maybe I picked the right thing

copyright

for you, maybe you wanted to smoke a cigarette for the last time."

"Well, what can I do? Can you leave me for ten minutes so I could smoke a cigarette in peace?" I said.

"Why not? But I will guard the house, don't think that you can run away."

He said this as he had his forefinger just below his eyes, pointing at me as he wanted to say: "Don't try anything stupid."

I was smoking the cigarette and pictures of my life were coming through my head. Birth, first days of life. I've experienced again the fear I've had when I saw my first teacher for the first time in my life.

That was the fear of entering the world, being surrounded by the people that weren't my family. After entering that social world, and after meeting so many people, I met a man who wanted to say that it was enough, I must leave this world now. I wasn't ready to leave because I didn't want to.

While pictures were coming through my head so fast that a cartoon movie could've

copyright

been made from them. When the pictures of the pain and the joy I felt crossed my mind, I remembered when a fire caught my left shoulder, it was a painful experience.

My shoulder is still covered with burn, and it will stay like that for life. I tattooed a picture of the fire on my right shoulder. I wanted to have something that will remind me that I can survive. No matter what happens in life, no matter how hard it gets, I can survive.

While I was thinking about all of that, I realized that I stored a cylinder full of gas in my cabinet. I decided to stub out stepping on the cigarette. I opened the cabinet and I pulled out the cylinder. I've set the cylinder behind the cabinet that was close to the chair that Edward had been sitting on. I let gas come out of the cylinder. Few minutes after that the room was full of gas. I opened the window to throw the cigarette butt. Edward was under the window.

"You want to run away? You've been thinking that I am stupid enough not to come under the window?" Just as he said that I threw the cigarette butt out of the window.

copyright

"No, I just wanted to get rid of this butt."

"Don't try to escape through exit door, because they're blocked. "

"Well, you were thinking about everything, didn't you?"

"I will be there in a few minutes. Get ready to die."

He came back to the room.

He pulled out his gun and he aimed it at me.

"Wait, can I know why are you doing this?"

"You know too much."

"Too much about what?"

"About underground world."

"So what If I do?"

"I don't want to risk. I know that you are planning to explore it. And once you get in touch with it, you will tell to others."

"And what If I do?"

copyright

"If you do, a plan is not going to work out."

"What kind of plan?"

Returning to the hospital

Chapter 7

He wanted to continue his speech with a cigarette in his mouth, so he put out the cigarette out of the box and he lighted it. Since the window was opened and wind was outside, he covered the lighter and the cigarette with his hand, so he could light it.

As soon as he put the cigarette in his mouth and bent his back looking at the floor, I jumped through the window. Just a few milliseconds after I jumped while I was still in the air, I heard the sound of explosion.

I was lying down there with my rib hurting like hell, but I was happy. It was good to be alive. I regained some strength and I continued walking. I went back to my house. I slept for 15 hours.

copyright

During my sleep, I was dreaming about Emma. In my dream, we were lying on a bed as she woke up shouting: "They're coming for me, save me please." I wanted to hug her but she just disappeared. The dream ended like that. As soon as I woke up I splashed my face with cold water. I lighted a cigarette as I was thinking about Emma. I decided it would be the best to go to the hospital and clear the things up.

I mean, I loved her, I didn't want that romance to end just like that. I took a taxi. As soon as I came to the hospital, I went to the room where she was hospitalized. In the same room, Edward was lying. I wasn't sure If I was still dreaming, so I slapped myself to ensure I was awake. I was awake and shocked. How come he survived? That is impossible.

He looked terrible. His face was burned, and the rest of his body was no different, except that it was wrapped in a bandage.

I had to make sure that it was him. I approached him.

"You motherfucker!" He mumbled. He wanted to stand up but the only thing that he

copyright

managed was was stretching out his hands. A female nurse came inside the room and put his hands down.

"Mr. Edward, you can't exert yourself! You need to rest,"

"And sir, who are you?" She added while looking at me.

"I have come to visit my girlfriend, but I can't see her here. You must have sent her to other room?"

"Yesterday in the morning when we came to examine her, she wasn't there. She just disappeared. We don't know what happened to her."

"What? How come nobody was there to guard the room?" I grabbed the nurse and yelled at her.

"Calm yourself down sir, please."

We called the police and they said that they will do their best to find her.

"But what if they don't find her? What if she has done something to herself?"

copyright

"I think you shouldn't panic sir"

"I can't believe this. You're so irresponsible." I said as I waved and left the hospital.

I knew that it had to do something with Edward. I had a total chaos in my head.

During the night, when everyone was sleeping, I went to the hospital in order to clear the things up with Edward.

Violence on the highway of desperation

Chapter 8

I approached his bed and slapped him few times in order to wake him up.

"I don't want my flakes now,"

"No one says that you're not cool, you're just not yourself," Edward murmured.

"Saying that you don't like your life makes you no better than the ones that died"

This man was saying strange things in his dream.

copyright

I didn't care much about what was he talking about. I slapped him few more time and he opened his eyes. You could've seen fear on his face. He was scared to death, but I didn't want to kill him. I just wanted to threaten him. I raised his head and I pulled out his pillow.

"You can't watch TV now you fried shit," I whispered

"You were thinking that you can kill me? A quiet man coming to drink to your pub must be harmless. Well, you were thinking wrong my friend." I added.

With my left hand, I grabbed the part of his bandage under his neck. I pulled the upper part of his body toward myself as I held his chin.

"Now you dipstick, tell me where is she?"

"I don't know who you are talking about." Said Edward with his slobbery mouth.

I took a tissue that was nearby and I wiped his mouth with it.

copyright

"Maybe spittle prevents you from remembering? Now spit it out, every word!"

"I said I don't know anything."

"Say it louder bitch!"

I put the pillow on his head.

"I'm not going to remove this pillow until you say it louder."

He muttered for a long time while his bed was shaking from the pressure of his body trying to remove the pillow from his head.

I've removed the pillow from his head and he took a deep breath few times.

"You see. I'm not even violent. I didn't hold that pillow not even a ten second on your head. Will you finally tell me what did you do with her and where is she?"

He took a plate from his table and hit my head with it. I fell on the floor. There were few drops of blood coming out of my nose. I have never been angrier in my life. I got up, cleaned the dust from my pants and I started punching him as hard as possible. I punched him 6 times.

copyright

I couldn't control myself. Next moment, he was unconscious. The device by him started buzzing. His life was in danger. As soon as I realized what I did I started running toward the exit. As I came closer to the doors of the room, I heard doctors talking and walking hurriedly towards the room. I hid behind the doors that were opened.

"Put it on 250!" Female doctor said. I was standing with my body against the wall. I heard an electric sound few times.

"We have him again. He's coming back" - Said the doctor.

"Wait, where is this blood coming from?" Asked doctor George whom I knew.

"Obviously from the nose." Answered female doctor.

"I see that, but I want to know who did this to Mr. Edward?"

"Mr. Edward is an asshole. This morning he touched my ass while I was giving him a medication."

"Well, maybe he is considering your ass as a relief for his soul." Doctor George said while he laughed.

"Fuck you and your humor. I will call the police. You stay here and look after him"

Taking back my love

Chapter 9

The female doctor got out of the room, and I was so glad that she didn't close the door because If she did, police wouldn't have to work this night that much and they wouldn't earn their salary in a fair manner.

Well, maybe I even cared a little bit about the fact that I could've been arrested. Anyway, she didn't close the door, and I was happy that she didn't.

I didn't know how to run away without being seen by the doctor, so I was standing there for the next 20 minutes. I looked around and I saw a stand and pills on it. I took a pill and I threw it so hard that it hit the window on the other side of the room. Doctor

copyright

George though it was someone from the outside. He hoped that it was the man they were looking for, the one that beat Edward.

Well, it was him, but from the inside. As doctor opened the window and looked around the trees and at the parking, searching for the subject that threw something on his window, I managed to exit the hospital without being seen.

I went back to my home. During my sleep, I was dreaming about Emma once again. This time she appeared in a red dress. She was walking to me. She held a yellow rose, tearing out the petals and throwing them in the air.

"Can't you see? They won't come into your hair. Does it mean that our love isn't strong enough? Where are you? Why don't you come? Who are you?"

Then she started crying. When I woke up I splashed my face with cold water and I stood in the bathroom for fifteen minutes looking in the mirror and trying to figure out if this dream had a special meaning.

copyright

I went back to the hospital to visit Edward once again.

"Not the pillow," He said as soon as I approached him.

"She's under the tree." He added.

"What tree?"

"Tree on the black ground that you saw moving."

I got out of the hospital, picked up a taxi and I went to the car service to see if my car was repaired, and luckily it was. I knew what I had to do, so I started the car and headed to the tree that Edward was talking about. I brought some water and food as I supposed that she was going to be exhausted. I was worried if she was going to recognize me because she might have lost her memory. I was even worried if she will talk to me, because of the car accident that I blamed myself for.

I've parked the car by the road, and I stepped my foot on the black even ground, I was walking three miles, but I couldn't see any tree. I was thinking that Edward deceived

copyright

me. Nevertheless, I continued walking. I walked so much that sweat covered my face completely. I've seen a small dot distanced about a mile from me. I started running.

When I was about to reach my destination, I started realizing that the dot was the tree, a black tree. When I came there, I saw her. My sweetheart Emma was tied against the tree. She was very exhausted.

"The tree above which birds don't fly," She said.

"Will you come and hug me, not the tree, please." She added.

I untied her, gave her the water to drink.

I sat myself down by her. I was hugging her while our backs were against the tree.

She started crying as she was talking how awful it was to be tortured.

"It was awful being inflicted all the pain, but it was even more painful coming through this without you,"

"Don't you ever leave me again, please." She added.

copyright

"Of Course I'm not going to leave you." I said as I kissed her forehead.

"Transmitting the neuro-signals trough invisible wires will not make sure that everyone gets affected. Yes Mr. Mark, but if the force is based..." Rest of the speech couldn't be heard.

"What the hell is this sound coming from the ground?" - I shouted.

"Since I'm tied here, I hear these voices." They're talking about destroying the world. They want to implement an idea in every human's brain.

"What kind of idea?"

"The idea of world's destruction, they want to make sure that humans destroy everything that is on the surface of the ground. They also want to make sure that humans destroy themselves."

"But aren't these voices under the ground voices of human beings?"

"Yes, they are normal people. They look just like me and you, but they are hidden and

copyright

nobody knows about them. Nobody but me, you, and Edward."

"When Edward found out that I know about the underground world, he kidnapped me. He brought me here, and he tied me to this tree. He said that he will send me to the underground world to be a part of them because letting me stay in the city is too risky. He didn't want anyone to reveal the secret of the world under the ground, that's why I'm lying here, waiting to be sent down there." She said while wiping a sweat that was on her forehead.

"I'm sorry, it was my fault. I should not have told him about our car accident. I told him that we had an accident because I was looking at something that was away from the road. As soon as I said this he realized that we saw the moving ground. He said: "Ground isn't always like that, is it?" Afterward, he denied that he knows anything about that. I realized that he regretted mentioning anything. He came to kill me, but I survived,"

copyright

"Maybe we should together go down there to see what's exactly happening?" She added.

"Don't you think that it's dangerous?" I asked her.

"Carl, the world is in our hands!"

"How do we get there?"

"Edward was talking about lighting."

"What kind of lighting?"

"Thunder has to stroke at this tree, and anyone who wants to go to the underground world must embrace this tree during the thunder stroke."

"But it's going to take a long time for the thunder to appear. If it's all about lighting, maybe we should burn this tree from the top to the bottom, and embrace the tree while standing on the ground, before the fire catches us."

"You're so fucking clever." She said while biting her lip.

copyright

Exploration of the bad side that underground world hides

Chapter 10

I started kissing her, and she put her hand in my pants.

She stepped back and she put her hair behind her ears.

"It's not the time for this now, we must control ourselves. We have a mission. We must save the world" She shouted.

"All right honey, I'll climb on this tree and light a fire, you stay down there, I'll come back soon."

I climbed the tree and after many tries, I managed to burn branches. I got back on the ground and I embraced the tree, and she did too. Since the tree wasn't so thick, I managed to put my hands around Emma. I was touching her from behind as she was giving off the sound of appreciation. All the sudden we were in a train wreckage. We were in a moving train wreckage. We've been traveling through some kind of wire, and inside the

copyright

wreckage, there were no seats. We were sitting on the iron. After few seconds of traveling the train stopped.

As soon as we stepped out of the train, we found ourselves in a dusty place with a green light. We could hardly see the things that surrounded us.

As we walked aimlessly we saw a door with the inscription on it "Industry of emotions, don't get in unless given the permission".

We've opened the door anyway. The door led us to a room, where we saw a screen that showed a man playing guitar with the rest of his band in front of a public. Public cheered as the leader of the band was jumping.

Next to that screen, there was another screen. This screen showed a short video of mother that just gave a birth to its child. The mother was smiling.

Next to that screen, there was a video that showed a man that was cleaning bird's excrement from his jacket. And the last one showed the sad man walking the street and

copyright

looking at the ruins of his city after the city was destroyed. A strange voice interrupted us while we were watching all of it.

"Why are you naked?" Asked a man that was wearing a white armor.

"We are not naked; can't you see that we have clothes on our bodies?" I said.

"I see that, but term "naked" in the underground world is used when one wants to say that someone is without emotion-resistant armor. Now get closer to one of the screens, and tell me what do you feel?" Said the man.

I was a bit afraid, but I approached the screen that was showing the man cleaning the bird's excrement from his jacket. I felt angry, the more I approached the screen, the angrier I was.

"Why do I feel so angry?" I asked the man.

"Because you're not wearing armor."

"What kind of armor?"

"The armor that I'm wearing. It protects you from being affected by the emotions of

copyright

other people. All of these videos that you can see here are showing a particular emotion. You feel angry because you've approached the screen showing an angry man that was hit by a bird's shit."

I stepped back from the screens.

"Okay, I get it now. But why do you have all of these screens here?"

"We're examining every emotion in order to make a human with a mindset that we want to have"

"What kind of human?" I asked.

"It's strange that you're not familiar with XLX2 project since you two are the models of our experiment. But it doesn't matter, you will receive the money for what you do even if you don't know what this is all about."

"You are wrong. We are no models; we came to live here under the ground."

"It's interesting. Do you want to get engaged in XLX2 project? Majority of the population of the underground world is participating in this project."

copyright

The world in a danger

Chapter 11

Emma and I were smart enough to know that pretending to be one of them will get us deeper into their plan, which will eventually be beneficial for our plan to save the world.

"People who live on the surface of the earth were given more than enough to make a good and happy life there. But you see that they didn't accomplish it. They were too stupid and too reckless to use all the resources successfully. We want to populate the earth after erasing the people that live on the surface. We have a plan how to make a good life, life without wars, without conflicts, a happy life. We are forming ways to change the human's mind. We have a plan to make a war that will make sure that every human being on the surface dies.

"Here, you can see the videos on the screens. Take a look at the walls. They are made of impulse wire. The wire is formed from the nerves taken from different animals,

copyright

the nerves are connected to the human being that is behind this wall. Every day one of our professionals go to the surface and kills a few animals.

Every time we renew a part of the wall by putting new nerves, screens reproduce other videos, showing other emotions. By replacing the nerves, we want to accomplish the best combination of emotions. We want to have four different emotions on four screens that are making a perfect combination. As an example, you've seen the video showing a man walking the street and looking at the ruins of his city. The man is sad.

We don't want sadness here. We want to see a proud man that walks the street and kills himself as a sign that last human from the surface is dead. And we want other three emotions to be different, to be beneficial to us. When we accomplish that, we will analyze the whole composition of neuro-system in the wall, and we will start making human beings with the same neuro-system.

Such human beings will be sent on the surface to make a mess. After they cause other people to destroy everything, including themselves, then we, people from the underground world are coming to the surface to make a good life.

"That sounds quite impressive." Says Emma.

"Now If you would please leave me alone, I am too busy working on the project." Said the man.

Planning of a murder and romance in the echo

Chapter 12

We got out of the room and we found a place where nobody could hear what we were talking about.

"It's fucked up here, isn't it? I said to Emma while I was holding both of my hands on the back of my head."

"We must stop XLX2!"

"How do we stop it?"

"Let's kill the man who is standing against the wall!"

copyright

"The one that has neuro-system of the wall connected to his body?"

"Yes, that one." - Emma affirmed.

"Let's search for the weapon."

"Where do we find it?" She asked

"How do you even know that they have weapons here?" She added.

"They are monstrous. If you're with me, take my hand and let me lead you."

We spent the whole day searching for a weapon. We couldn't find it.

"Why don't you just quit, there are no weapons here, not even a sharp object. How do you think you're going to kill him?"

"I don't know, I'm stressed out."

As soon as I said this, Emma started kissing me. Almost every room that we've been through was covered with a light. This room was a combination of green and red light. She stripped me off as we were at the place where red and green light were combined. I was lying on the ground as she touched every part of my body with her lips leaving traces of a lipstick, shaped in a circle, and hot like an eye full of curiosity.

I was lying on my belly and she was giving me a massage. She spread her legs and she started giving me a massage from my neck all the way to my legs. That little part between her legs provided me with so much of pleasure that I couldn't help myself not to have it on my tongue.

She didn't hesitate to provide me with the same pleasure. I was upside down while she was in the normal position. We've been like that for 30 minutes.

Fluids that were coming out of our bodies were the ones that nobody produced ever before. Feeling it in my lower body she was jumping on me like the sex could save the world. With my strength regained and full of adrenaline I made her love not letting her move from me. I led her trough the world of pain and pleasure and it led to orgasm. Lying on the wet floor I asked her If she had enough.

copyright

"My feminine need will never make me feel like I had enough.

But you're tough enough to provide me with some more, aren't you?"

"Of Course I am."

I made her love for the whole night. We did it so many times that last few times her body produced blood, but she was okay.

Unexpected direction of bullets

Chapter 13

In the morning, we were walking through the underground world. Underground world was so huge that one would have to walk for days to see all of it.

We were at the main place, in the industry of emotions. We walked toward the main room of the industry of emotions, the one where the man was connected to the neuro-system built in the wall. As we came closer to the room, we've seen a guard with a gun by his waist. I looked at Emma and I hugged her.

copyright

"Remember this: I'm alive even if I die."

Just as I said this, I approached the guard from his back and I pulled out the gun from his waist. I shot him in his back as I ran toward the wall man. I put the gun in his mouth. The next moment gunshot resounded. I feel dead on the floor. Edward shot me in my head from my back.

"He who dares wins. Since both of us dared, one had to be smarter. That was me, my friend. I won."

Said Edward, as Emma hugged my dead body. This time my body produced blood, and cause of the blood wasn't love.

If I knew that this time I was going to die and If I had a chance to choose my last wish, I would've chosen to spend one more day helping my patients with a sound of guitar. My life was hard.

This time it wasn't hard for me to lie on the floor since I didn't feel anything. It was hard for her to look at my dead body. If I could somehow feel something for the last time while I was lying dead on the floor, I

copyright

would've felt a regret, regret of not being able to cure my sweetheart.

Journey to the nest of fear

Chapter 14

Emma didn't want to save the world anymore because what meant the world to her, couldn't be saved anymore. She found out that there is a good side of the underground world, and two months after I died she moved to the better side of the underground world.

This part of the underground world is also based on production of emotions. The underground world Emma moved to was called "sphere 2".

The first people that populated the earth were the ones residing in underground space. Thanks to them, people on the surface have emotions today. People from Sphere 2 are developing the emotions since a first man stepped on the surface with his foot.

copyright

At the entrance to the sphere 2, one is given the power to fly. Emma was flying until she came to the good side. At the good side, white color prevailed. The first thing that Emma saw when she landed on the good side was a rap battle.

The people that worked at the entrance of the sphere 2 were engaged to supply the surface with compassion. There is a lot of compassion in rap music. The people that worked there rapped as much as possible distributing inspiration trough invisible wire.

Next that she saw was a group of people playing the violin. This place of the sphere 2 was called soothing. She wandered the sphere 2. She would often think about me. She was thinking about all the nights we spent together. She was thinking about how she hoped to have a child with me.

Her world was covered with sadness. Coming through negative emotions of the sphere 2, she would be thinking about how she feels now. But going through positive emotions of the sphere 2, she would remember all the beautiful moments she had

copyright

with me. When she came to the laboratory of sadness she started crying. A woman that worked there hugged her.

"What's wrong, you beautiful woman?" She asked Emma.

"The Idea that people can die is wrong. Why do we die anyway?"

"Death is also a part of the life. Without death, there is no life. Without life, there is no death. Without marriage, there is no divorce, and without divorce, there is not a little child missing one of its parents."

"Who have you lost?"

"I've lost my boyfriend."

"Did you love him?

"More than anything."

"Come here, I will show you what it's like when sadness rains on the world."

She was coming through the room and she was seeing the pictures so sad that they were wet all the time, incapable of getting dried as if the pictures were crying

copyright

themselves. The first picture that she saw was a man in a suit lying on the ground while a woman in a wedding dress tries to awake him. It was a man that experienced a heart attack just when he wanted to say "Yes".

"Colleagues from thrill department made this fault. They've developed excitement so much that some people ended up dying because they were too thrilled."

The next picture she showed to Emma was the picture of destroyed city after it was bombed. On the picture, there was a kid peering with his head just as he wanted to say: "Is it over? Can we get out of shelter now and get beck to our home?" Unfortunately, there was no home. How should one feel in such moment? A bird without a place to spend most of its time there is a bird set free, but a man without a house is a caged man.

"How come you have these pictures from the surface?" Emma asked.

"We have people that go up there and they take pictures of situations that led to sadness."

copyright

"Thank you for showing me these pictures." Said Emma.

She was wandering the sphere 2. It was so white that at the moment she was thinking that snow was surrounding her. All the sudden a motorbike approached her and asked her if she is going to the department of love.

She said that she is walking aimlessly, but that she would be glad to visit the department of love.

"Why are you going there?" She asked the man.

"Because I want to know about that beautiful emotion. By the way, I've lost my girlfriend not a long time ago and I want to know if there's something that I've ever missed to give her in our love. She killed herself, so I want to know If I've made a mistake in the love and if I've been a reason why she killed herself."

"Oh, that's so sad, but don't blame yourself. Nobody is perfect. I bet she did it for some other reason that can't be related to

copyright

you... By the way, not long time ago I've lost a boyfriend." Said she.

They talked a lot, since the department of love was far away.

When they came there, they split. One of the women that worked there started showing pictures on the wall to Emma. There was a picture where I was making love to Emma in the garden. She didn't know whether to smile or to cry when she saw that. Anyway, she didn't want to ask how come they have that picture, since she was already told that people from sphere 2 have to go on the surface to see how do emotions that they developed work. She showed her pictures of births and pictures of most romantic kisses.

"Do you know where the department of fear is?"

"Are you sure that you want to go there? The man that works there is not so nice. It's a very depressive place.

"I'm sure, I want to go there!"

"Then just lead this road, and when you see that light is not as white as it is here, you

copyright

will know that you've reached the destination."

"Thank you very much."

When she entered the door of the department of fear, it was almost completely dark. Only half of the room was bright. A bold man with a big scar on his cheek was sitting by the table.

"What's your name?" Asked the man.

"My name is Emma."

"May I help you?"

"You can't even help yourself."

"How do you mean that?"

"I've tried so many times to get rid of the phobia, but you never wanted to make it easier. You were scared and therefore unable to help yourself overcome your fear of helping, so you could help others beat their fears."

"You know what? You don't deserve any help, you deserved that fear. One day you will realize."

copyright

"I'm tired of waiting. I'm tired of figuring out the things."

As soon as she said this she pulled out a gun and tried to shoot the bold man. In the moment when she pulled the trigger, two wolves emerged from nowhere and they ran one to another so fast that they were intersected in the moment when the bullet was supposed to shoot the bold man. Instead of shooting the man, both of wolves were killed.

"You see. There is a difference between good and the bad underground world.

In the bad underground world, animals are producing negative emotions. In this good world where we form emotions and distribute it to the surface, we let a man not get killed because of the black magpies he painted.

And we let the producer of all the fears including your phobia not to die because wolfs decided to intersect themselves. You killed the cause of your fears and now I will kill you."

copyright

The bald man pulled out a gun and shot her five times right in her heart.

The persistence of wolves

Chapter 15

At the end, she came to the deepest place in the earth. It's called third dimension. That is a place where people with the highest intensity of lust lived. Animals didn't live there, only people did. As soon as she saw me she jumped on me and hugged me. We didn't talk much. I was kissing her with so much of lust that everyone from third dimension would envy me, and the competition was tough.

I've lifted her and set her in the position so that her back was against the wall.

I gave her more kisses than life gave us troubles. She was wearing a skirt with no underwear. The fire between us was so high that I couldn't resist but to make it up to her by going as hard as possible.

copyright

She was screaming like never before but she didn't want me to stop. After fifteen minutes, we were both naked on the floor.

She talked about how she wanted to commit a suicide, and how glad was she that she got killed. She was glad to be with me once again, and I was glad to be with her. This time it was forever, there was no reason to leave this place. As we talked about what has she been through, we heard a prolonged sound of explosion.

"The world is destroyed. The bad dimension of the underground world achieved what they planned. There is nobody alive on the surface, and it will stay like that until people from the underground go to build a new life there." I said.

Emma was talking about how she killed two wolves while they were intersected, saying that the wolves that she saw on the TV were intersected when her phobia emerged.

Few second after she said that we heard a growling sound.

"What's this?"

copyright

"Can't you see? Wolves will never die." I whispered as I continued making love to her.

copyright

I write under the pseudonym: Urquhart Randolph. I like to write great romance stories that take you on a blazing journey - tears, laughter (may be both) or just a steamy hot fun (perhaps all of them).

Please... leave a review, regardless if you think my book deserves 1* or 5 * let me know if you had enjoyed this great story?

THANK YOU ☺

VISIT US
WWW.GLOFTON.COM
Enroll in our VIP list.
Be the first to be notified on our latest published book.
Downloading for free gifts.

www.ingramcontent.com/pod-product-compliance
Lightning Source LLC
Chambersburg PA
CBHW020648130626
46552CB00003B/1449

* 9 7 8 1 9 4 6 7 9 2 0 7 5 *